CARTER'S
COLORFUL JOURNEY

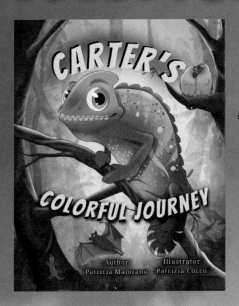

+

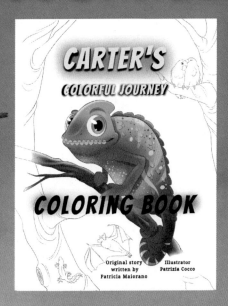

Also available
from this Author

amazon

I dedicate this book to my parents Angela and Giovanni Maiorano, the real lovebirds. From their everlasting love for each other to the love and kindness they spread amongst family and friends, they have touched the hearts of everyone they ever met. I want to honor them by making them heroic characters in my story. They were my true life heroes.

Designer & Formatter Jo Blake

ISBN: 9798781535859

CARTER'S

COLORFUL JOURNEY

Patricia Maiorano

Illustrator

Patrizia Cocco

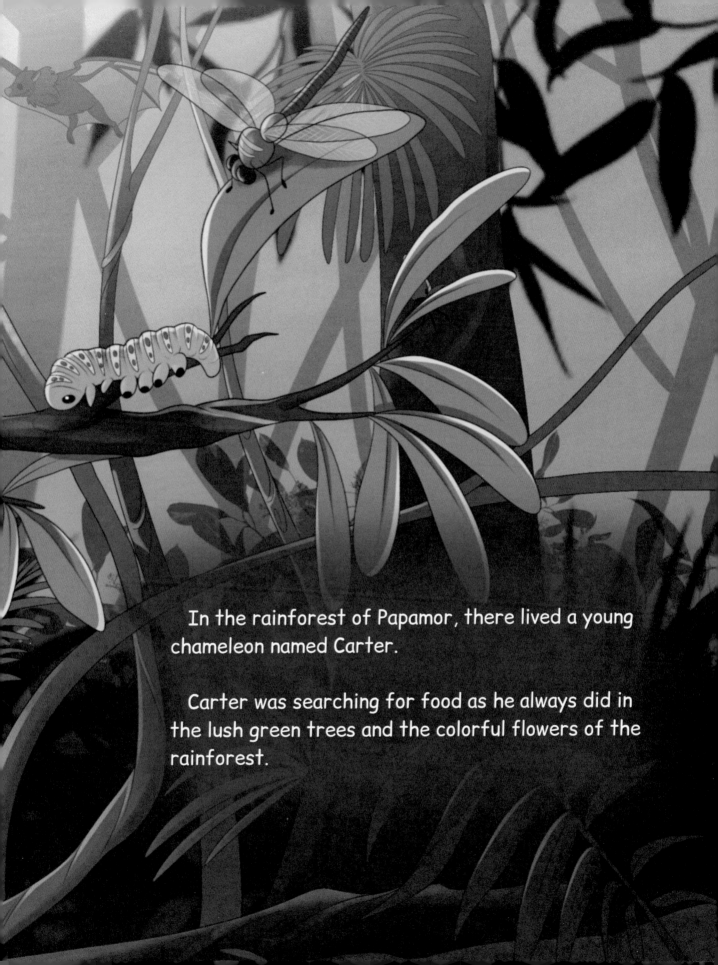

In the rainforest of Papamor, there lived a young chameleon named Carter.

Carter was searching for food as he always did in the lush green trees and the colorful flowers of the rainforest.

Carter was so hungry and distracted, he hopped onto Freddy Fruit Bat's branch by accident. Freddy Fruit Bat was hanging out with Larry the Lying Lizard.

Carter gasped. "Oh, hello," he said.

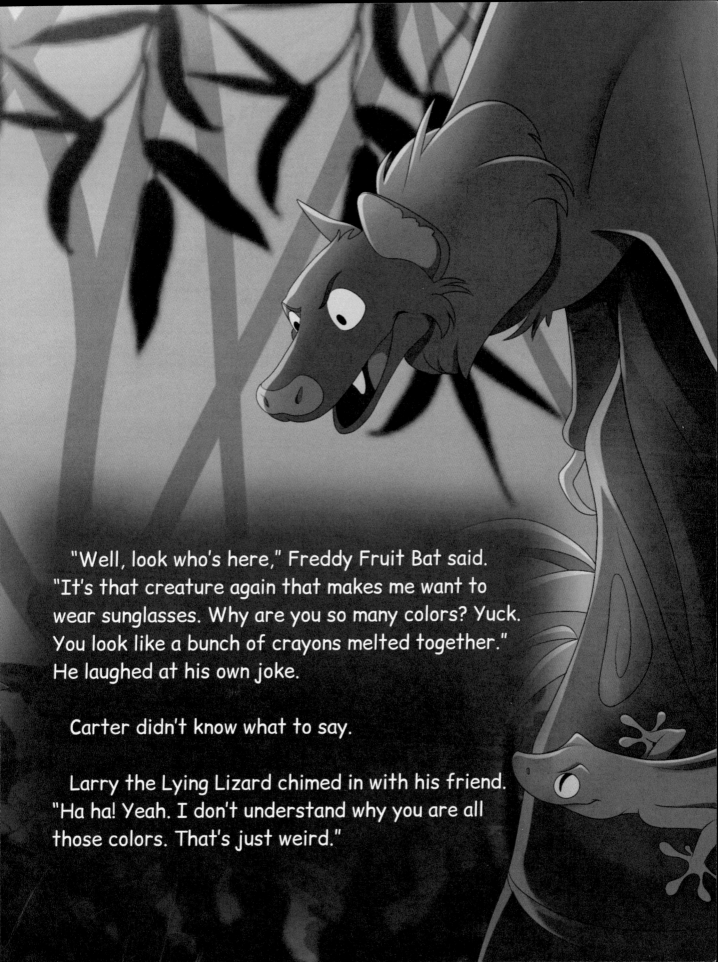

"Well, look who's here," Freddy Fruit Bat said. "It's that creature again that makes me want to wear sunglasses. Why are you so many colors? Yuck. You look like a bunch of crayons melted together." He laughed at his own joke.

Carter didn't know what to say.

Larry the Lying Lizard chimed in with his friend. "Ha ha! Yeah. I don't understand why you are all those colors. That's just weird."

Carter jumped away from them, but he couldn't get their words or laughter out of his head. He felt so bad about his colors that he went to one far away branch and camouflaged himself.

He did not want anyone else to notice his ability to change color to match his surroundings. He didn't want other creatures to think he was weird.

So, Carter stayed on the branch to think and to try to stay one color.

"Why would that Freddy and Larry make fun of me?" Carter asked himself. "Don't they know that's not nice?"

As Carter's emotions changed from sadness to anger, he noticed that he couldn't even stay one color if he held still. How he felt in his heart showed on his skin.

"What am I going to do?" Carter moaned. "I can't stay here in one place!"

The next morning, he woke up on the same branch. He remembered the teasing.

Carter started to cry. "I just don't know how I can fix this," he said.

Just then, he saw two birds fly by. Carter stopped crying and was on high alert! He did not want to become their prey.

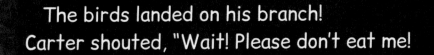

The birds landed on his branch!
Carter shouted, "Wait! Please don't eat me!

"Don't be afraid of us," one of the colorful birds said.
"We heard you crying and wanted to help."

"My name is Gio," said the first bird.

"My name is Lina," said the other bird.

"What is your name?"

"Carter," the little chameleon whispered.

Lina continued, "Are you hungry? It seems like you haven't found much food here."

"Yes," said Carter. "I am hungry. I tried catching food but I'm too upset and the fly saw my colors come through. I thought I could stay still and not be seen."

Gio laughed a little. "Then why don't you just move?"

Lina shushed Gio. "Would you like to tell us why you are staying on this branch?"

"Some creatures were saying stuff..." Carter sniffed.

"What did they say?"

"That my colors are weird."

Lina and Gio ruffled their colorful feathers. "Who said that?!" said Lina.

"Who could think such a thing?" said Gio.

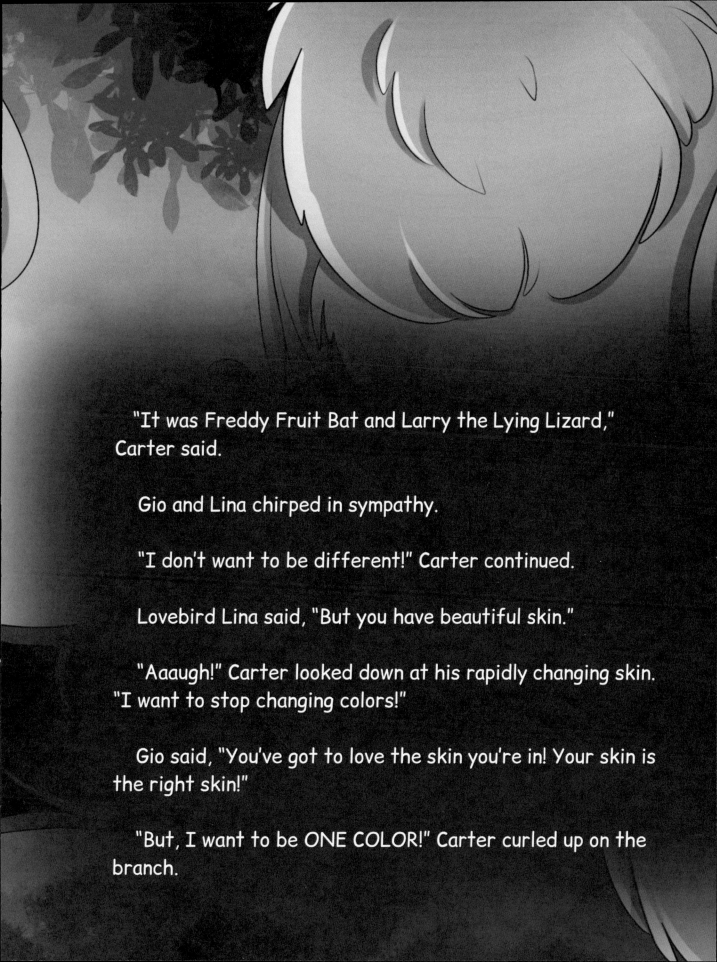

"It was Freddy Fruit Bat and Larry the Lying Lizard," Carter said.

Gio and Lina chirped in sympathy.

"I don't want to be different!" Carter continued.

Lovebird Lina said, "But you have beautiful skin."

"Aaaugh!" Carter looked down at his rapidly changing skin. "I want to stop changing colors!"

Gio said, "You've got to love the skin you're in! Your skin is the right skin!"

"But, I want to be ONE COLOR!" Carter curled up on the branch.

Lovebird Lina whispered something to Gio.

"Ah, yes! Great idea!" Gio said. "Carter, have you ever been east of Papamor?"

"No, why?" Carter asked.

"There is a chameleon named Camilla who lives in that area," Lina said. "She is a special chameleon that cannot change her colors."

Gio added, "Would you like to meet her? We could go right now!"

"What for?" Carter asked.

Gio said, "Let's just say she has certain challenges because she can't change colors like you do."

"Ok," Carter said. "I guess I can meet her."

As they approached the east part of Papamor, they saw Camilla. Lina, Gio and Carter sensed something was wrong and did not call out to her.

Camilla leapt up to their branch. A few seconds later a snake slithered by.

"Whew, that was close!" exclaimed Carter.

The lovebirds introduced Camilla to Carter the Chameleon.

Hi, I'm Camila. What beautiful colors you have!

"Thanks," said Carter.

"Your colors must help you hide in many different places," Camila said.

"Yes, but I look like a bunch of melted crayons and that's weird!"

"What are crayons?" Camila asked.

"I don't know," Carter said. "That's what some creatures said."

I think your colors are beautiful," Camila said, "like a rainbow or the flowers you find in this rainforest! They aren't just beautiful, though, I bet they are useful! How do you use them?"

"Well, when I hold very still, I match wherever I am."

"Yeah, and tasty meals come right up to me because they don't see me. But if I am feeling scared or excited, my colors change."

Wow, that must be so cool!" said Camina. "I use my eyes and very good hearing to help me find food. I have to be really quick out here. I also dance and move like the leaves."

"Camila, thank you for teaching me to like myself the way I am. I want to be friends with you."

"Thank you, Carter, for being my friend. I think we can help each other. We can work together with our strengths!"

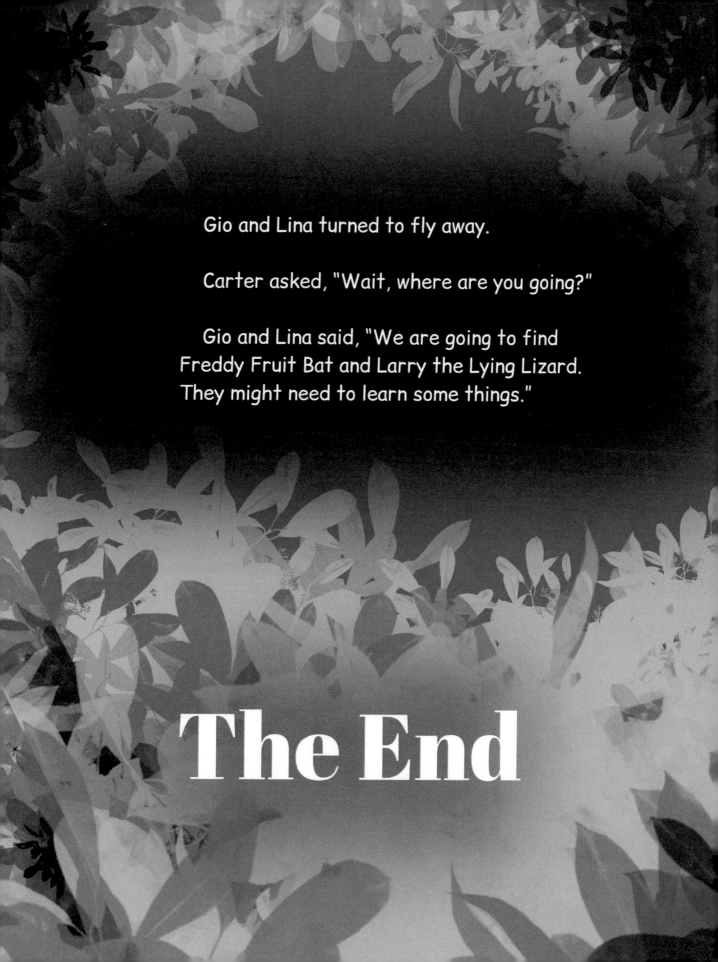

Gio and Lina turned to fly away.

Carter asked, "Wait, where are you going?"

Gio and Lina said, "We are going to find
Freddy Fruit Bat and Larry the Lying Lizard.
They might need to learn some things."

The End

Did You Know?

1. Chameleons mostly live in a place called Madagascar.

2. Chameleons have skin crystals that enable them to change color at will.

3. Chameleons can change their colors when they need to control their body temperature.

4. They can also change their colors in order to show their emotions. You can say that they wear their emotions on their skin.

5. Chameleons have a distinctive back and forth kind of walk. This interesting kind of walk helps chameleons to imitate swaying leaves.

6. Chameleons have eyes that can swivel and move in two different directions at once.

7. Their hands and feet work like salad tongs to clamp down on a branch.

8. Their tails wrap around trees to balance.

9. Chameleons' long tongues can reach anything twice their body length and catch an insect.

10. Chameleons' saliva is very sticky. This helps them pull in their food.

About The Author

Patricia Maiorano is a second-time children's book author. She has been an educator for over 20 years. She loves writing stories from her heart. She hopes the messages in her stories will inspire and reach her students and other children beyond the classroom. She speaks three languages and plans to translate her books into those languages. When Patricia is not teaching or writing, she spends her days with family and friends. She loves to cook the Traditional Italian meals her mom has taught her throughout the years. She loves to dance, travel and learn new musical instruments to play. Her favorite hobby of all is spoiling her dog named Sadie. Please look for more information on Patricia's social media pages for upcoming books.

Follow me on social media

Facebook - www.facebook.com/PatriciaMaiorano
Instagram - www.instagram.com/leftylady74
Tic Tok - www.tictok.com/leftlady16
Twitter- www.twitter.com/leftylady74

Illustrator

Illustrator Patrizia Cocca was born in in Cagliari in Italy. She has been passionate about drawing since childhood, loving it so much that over the years she deciding to follow it as a profession. Patrizia had always dreamed of illustrating children's books, so she studied by herself with the help of books.

"I would like to tell children who will read this book and see my drawings, never give up on your dreams!"

Follow me on social media

Facebook - www.faceboo.com/PatriziaCoccoArt
Instagram - www.instagram.com/patriziacocco94

Designer and formattor

Jo Blake lives in Devon, England with her family and pets. She has always loved children's books and how they can support social emotional well being. An artist, illustrator, author and designer herself, Jo has always loved to draw and create from a young age.

"Find your talent, a way of connecting with people. By being yourself, you will find the power to - Shine!"

Follow me on social media

Website - www.joblakeart.co.uk
Facebook / instagram /twitter - @joblakeart

Acknowledgements

To the most talented, brilliant illustrator, Patrizia Cocco. I was so lucky to have you illustrate my story with true works of art. You have exceeded my expectations with all the vibrant colors. You made my characters come alive with such perfection in conveying my story. Disney would be proud!

To my friend/designer/formatter Jo Blake. I have so much gratitude for the creativity, patience and expertise you have. I am so pleased to have an award-winning author, illustrator and designer be part of my book. You did an amazing job in bringing my book together!

A million thank yous! To the great editor, Heidi Cook! I thank you for bringing your guidance and knowledge to my project. You have made an impact in shaping my story into what it is today!

To the man who continues to motivate me and inspire me to keep following my dreams, Andrew Ramirez. I will forever be grateful for taking your workshops!

To my best friend Maria, thank you for your unwavering support and great ideas that I have incorporated into my books. Thank you for always being there through it all! Hope to see your book written one day as well!

I also want to thank my family and friends who have been there for me with their love and support and continue to cheer me on along this literary journey of mine.
Thank you!

Last but not least, to my readers. I hope this book will inspire you to be a person who embraces who they are and to want to be a better person. Acceptance of every kind of human, whether they look the same as you or different. More love, not hate. Being kind, helpful and loving is the kind of world we want to leave for our future generations.

Patricia Maiorano

Made in the USA
Middletown, DE
30 May 2022

66312845R00020